For my Flea

First U.S. edition 2009

Library of Congress Cataloging-in-Publication Data is available.
Library of Congress Catalog Card Number 2008929161
ISBN 978-0-7636-4243-3

2 4 6 8 10 9 7 5 3

Printed in China

This book was typeset in Malonia Voigo.
The illustrations were done in pencil crayon and chalk pastel.

Candlewick Press
99 Dover Street,
Somerville, Massachusetts 02144

visit us at www.candlewick.com

SEYMOUR and HENRY

Kim Lewis

CANDLEWICK PRESS

Seymour and Henry played in the pond.

Plop, went Seymour.

Plop, went Henry.

All day long they swam
with Mommy.

Then Mommy flapped her wings.
"Come along, my little ducks,"
she said. "It's time for us
to go home."

But the ducklings kept on playing.

They didn't want to stop.

"Quack!" said Seymour.

"Quack!" said Henry.

They ran away from Mommy.

Pit-a-pat, went Seymour.

Pit-a-pat, went Henry.

Seymour hopped
up onto a log.

Henry wriggled
under.

Seymour scampered
around a rock.

Around and around

ran Henry.

The ducklings ran a little farther.

Pit-a-*pat*, they scampered—

through tall grass

and down a hill.

Slippy-slidey-bump,

they landed.

Then the little

ducklings hid.

"Quack!"
giggled Seymour.
"Quack!"
giggled Henry.

They waited
for Mommy
to come and
find them.

They waited.

And waited.

Plip, plop, came
some drops of rain.
They fell on
Seymour's head.

Plip, plop,
more drops came.
They fell on
Henry, too.

Plip-plop, plip-plop, the rain fell down.

"QUACK!" the ducklings cried.

Pit-a-pat, went Seymour.

Pit-a-pat, went Henry.

Up the hill,

through

the grass,

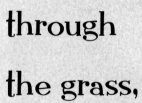

around

the rock,

and under

the log.

They ran as fast as they could go.

And there was Mommy, waiting for them.

"Quack!" said Seymour.

"Quack!" said Henry.

Plip-plop, plip-plop, went the rain.

The little ducklings skipped
and danced.

Then Mommy flapped her wings.

"Come along, my little ducks," she said.

"Hop on for a ride."

"Quack!" sang Seymour.

"Quack!" sang Henry.

And *pit-a-pat, pit-a-pat* . . .

Mommy took her
ducklings home.